JIMMY LEE DID IT

BY PAT CUMMINGS

HarperTrophy
A Division of HarperCollins*Publishers*

Jimmy Lee is back again
And nothing is the same.

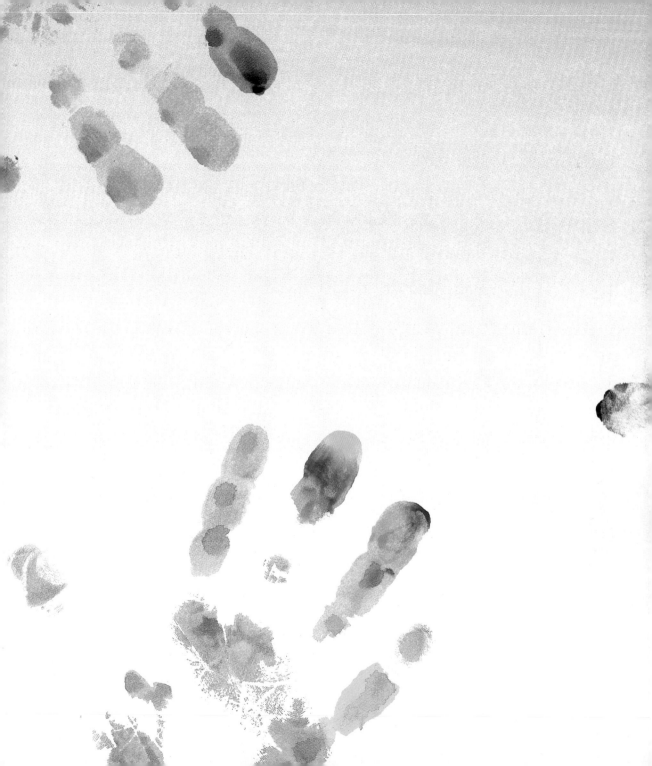

To Angel and the Crampo Kid

---

and with special thanks to Barbara Lalicki

Jimmy Lee Did It
Copyright © 1985 by Pat Cummings
All rights reserved. No part of this book may be used or reproduced in any manner whatsoever without written
permission except in the case of brief quotations embodied in critical articles and reviews. Printed in Mexico. For
information address HarperCollins Children's Books, a division of HarperCollins Publishers, 10 East 53rd Street,
New York, NY 10022.
Published by arrangement with Lothrop, Lee & Shepard Books, a division of William Morrow & Company, Inc.
LC Number 84-21322
Trophy ISBN 0-06-443357-9
First Harper Trophy edition, 1995.

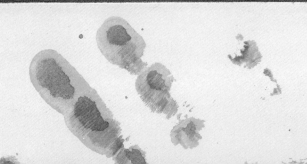

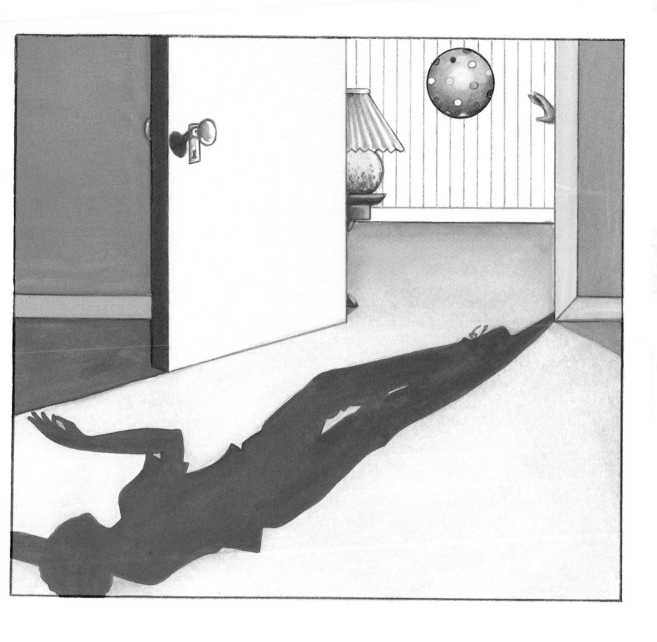

He's causing lots of trouble,
While my brother takes the blame.

Artie made his bed, he said.
But Jimmy thinks he's smart.

While Artie read his comics,
Jimmy pulled the sheets apart.

Dad fixed us pancakes
And Artie said his tasted fine,

But Jimmy Lee had just been there
And eaten most of mine.

I heard the crash of breaking glass,
But turned too late, I guess.

"Jimmy Lee did it," Artie said,
As we cleaned up the mess.

When Artie's room got painted,
Jimmy Lee was in the hall.

He used up Artie's crayons
Drawing pictures on the wall.

And when I finally found my bear,
I asked Artie, "Who hid it?"

He told me frankly, "Angel,
It was Jimmy Lee who did it."

He caused so much trouble
That I began to see—

The only way to stop it
Was to capture Jimmy Lee.

I knew about his sweet tooth,
So I set a tasty trap,

But Jimmy Lee just waited
Till I had to take my nap.

I spread out all my marbles
To trip up Jimmy Lee.

The dog slid by and scratched the floor
And Mom got mad at me.

I hid in the hall closet
And I never made a sound,

But Jimmy Lee will only come
When Artie is around.

I don't know what he looks like,
He never leaves a trace—

Except for spills and tears
And Artie's things about the place.

Since Artie won't describe him,
He remains a mystery.

But if you're smart, you'll listen
And watch out for Jimmy Lee.

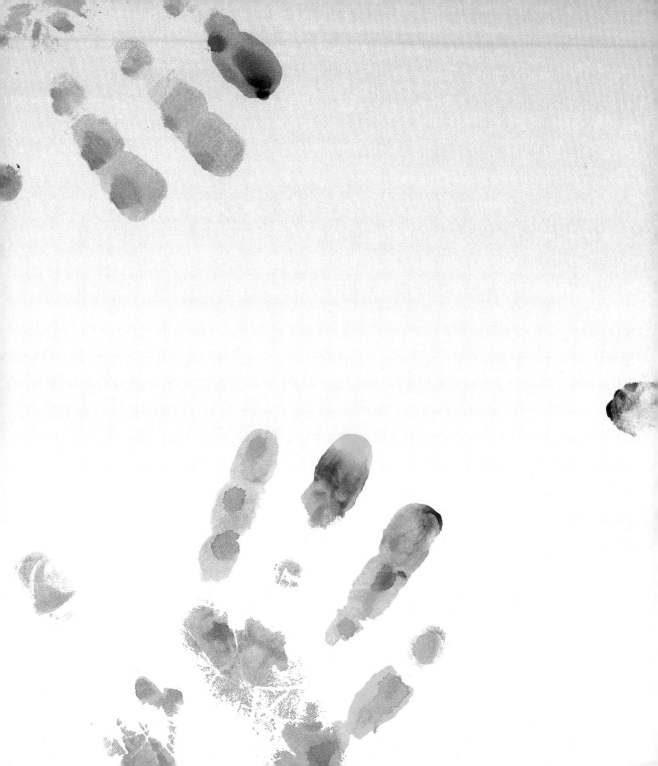